Purple and Blue

Laurel Bell-Krasner

iUniverse, Inc.
New York   Bloomington

Purple and Blue

This is a work of fiction. All of the characters, names, incidents,
organizations, and dialogue in this novel are either the products
of the author's imagination or are used fictitiously.

iUniverse books may be ordered through booksellers or by contacting:

iUniverse
1663 Liberty Drive
Bloomington, IN 47403
www.iuniverse.com
1-800-Authors (1-800-288-4677)

Because of the dynamic nature of the Internet, any Web addresses or
links contained in this book may have changed since publication and
may no longer be valid. The views expressed in this work are solely
those of the author and do not necessarily reflect the views of the
publisher, and the publisher hereby disclaims any responsibility for
them.

ISBN: 978-1-4502-3078-0 (sc)
ISBN: 978-1-4502-3079-7 (ebook)

Printed in the United States of America

iUniverse rev. date: 06/15/2010

Special Thanks To:
Lauren Conrad & Stephen Colletti
For Laguna Beach, Episode 201.
And for All the Great Times That We Could Relate to.
Emirem
For the Inspiration and Always Being There for Me to
Keep Me Focused and Thinking Clearly.
Thank You For Continuing to Sacrifice Having a
Normal Life for Your Fans. We Love You, Man.
And Michael Jackson
For Motivating Me with Your Brilliance and Teaching
Me to do Everything with L.O.V.E.
We Really Miss You.

For Sean

I have faith in everything you do. You have more potential than anyone I have ever known. I wish that I could make you a halo out of the greenest blades of grass, but I have failed miserably in my every attempt to make jewelry out of blades of grass. Life isn't perfect, but that's ok because sometimes even the mistakes happen for a reason. It's ok that we can't give a hundred percent to the world every day. Sometimes emotions get in the way, and sometimes, if we are lucky, that ends up being the best thing anyway. I did not give a hundred percent of my writing skills to this book. But I put it together in one weekend for you because I saw it as my only option, and without you, not one word of it would exist. Not one word. I swear to God. You have given the world this story that you will see really is partially yours. What I have learned is that if we want to be moral, we must make the conscious decision to do what is right every day, even when we can't give that a hundred percent of our effort. I think you know what is true and what isn't. Artists (including writers and musicians) are not paid for our work and maybe not even our talent. Sean, we are paid for our vision, because we can see what others can't and we find a way to translate it into a language they can understand. I admit that this wasn't the goal of this book, and that's why it ends the way it does. It had to be believable, but I know you understand. And I know that you have a "beautiful" vision. Every day is a present. Please do not be afraid, and do not waste your time worrying or trying to be the best. As far as many people are concerned, you already are. You are the emerald in so many people's eyes. You inspire me to work half as hard as you do. Whatever you do, don't ever stop being you. And remember, the three of us are still here, but that's a miracle. I will always thank God for your every precious breath.

There is no tomorrow/Just some picture perfect day/ That lasts a whole lifetime /And it never ends.

– Shawn Carter

If you wanna make the world a better place/Take a look at yourself and then make that change!

– Michael Jackson

Based on a true story.
Some names have been changed to protect identities.

<u>Chapter 1</u>

It was a beautiful summer day in New England. Not too hot. Just nice. And with the sun clearly shining. On a green, grassy hill there are a few fourteen year-olds looking up at the puffy clouds. A boy named Jeff sits next to a girl in a skimpy brown tank top. Jeff says to her, "that one looks like the leaning tower of pizza!" She giggles and looks at him, before looking up again. She points and exclaims to him, "that one looks like a pear!" He laughs. A few feet away, a girl named Laurel waves away the boys who surround her and whispers to another girl.

"Did you hear that?" she asks the other girl.

"Hear what?"

"His laughter."

The other girl glares at Laurel.

"You're being weird. You don't even know them."

"Ok well the only reason he is with her is because of her boobs."

"Somebody's jealous."

"I am not jealous."

"Then why do you care?"

"I don't know yet. There's something about his laughter that belongs to me. And he's beautiful, isn't he?"

Chapter 2

Jeff and Laurel are the last ones to walk back from where they're supposed to be after the hill. She runs to catch up with him.

"Hey!"

He turns around.

"Hey."

"Um, I'm Laurel. What's your name?"

He takes her hand and introduces himself.

"I'm Jeff."

Laurel notices something in his eyes.

"Wow, you have really pretty eyes. And I can tell even under that baseball cap that you have great hair."

He's uneasy, so she says, "So that girl you were just sitting with is probably your girlfriend, and that's cool, but do you think maybe we can hang out sometime? Just as friends?" He tells her, "Definitely," and they begin to walk back together. She is interested in finding out anything she can about him, but decides she better not freak him out. She learns that he plays soccer, and he learns that she wears her emotions on her sleeve, or at least in her expression. He silently thinks to himself that this girl does not have a poker face. But he notices something special about her. Like maybe she can lie, but maybe it's only him who can see right through it. Since he can tell that she isn't interested in soccer, he offers his piano-playing skills as an alternative for discussion. She's instantly hooked. They have to leave each other to go back to their groups, which are separated by gender. They throw each other a "later," but can still see each other from where they're sitting. She can't stop stealing glances at him when she thinks he isn't looking.

Chapter 3

One Week Later

Jeff and Laurel see each other on the Quad. Jeff walks up to her with that familiar smirk and maybe he has a poker face, but he wants her to know what's going on, so he decidedly almost can't keep from laughing. She asks him what he's up to, and then wishes she hadn't. "I'm about to go stick tennis balls down my shirt and get my nails painted. Wanna come?" She just stares at him in something that is not quite shock and tells him she doesn't know why she bothers. Later, when he's nowhere around, she laughs about all of this to herself. There is something about it that it so far from perfect and yet so right.

One week after that, Jeff and Laurel are hugging each other. She looks up at him and sadly says, "We're going to different schools." He tells her that she worries too much. The only thing she can think to say in response is "Jeff." There is something special between them, but it will not be until years later that they will figure out what any of it could possibly mean. They recognize each other's expressions as if they are their own. He can see that she is pained. So he holds her hips for a moment and replies "Laurel."

Chapter 4

One Month Later

Laurel and Jeff have entered ninth grade at separate schools. Laurel is doing homework. She stares at her clock for a moment in disbelief. The green digital numbers are telling her that it is sometime around midnight and she's still drinking Coke and trying to finish geometry homework. She sheds two tears and picks up her cell to call Jeff. He continues playing video games while he talks to her.

"I don't understand this. I give up."

Jeff understands and says, "Don't give up. Just give up for tonight. Go to bed. Don't let this bother you."

"But my head hurts so bad!"

"Just go to bed."

She flips her cell shut, leaves her math book open with her homework papers on the floor, and climbs under her purple covers with her clothes on.

<u>Chapter 5</u>

Jeff and Laurel are on their cell phones with each other. She apparently has to tell him something. He listens. She begins, "Well, for English class we had to make up a story about our futures. Just like, a paragraph. And we only had class time to do it, so I had to focus so I didn't get sent to do a lap again, and all I could focus on was you. So I wrote about how we're going to get married. And um, I had to read it to the class."

Jeff laughs to her, "Oh, Laurel."

She's content that he isn't really bothered by it, and she changed the subject.

"So how's soccer?"

"It's good. It's really good. I got two goals this week."

"Cool. English has been fun. I mean, I get sent to do laps a lot, like when I ask questions unrelated to the discussion, or when she can tell I'm thinking about you. But it's like our classroom is a home to come back to. We talk about everything with each other, but for me it's hard because she always makes me read like a page more out loud than everyone else, I guess because I'm a good reader."

"That's good."

"It's fine. I just don't like when we do vocab. You'd be surprised how much of that I get wrong. But I know she's just trying to help us with PSATs."

"Yeah well at least you don't have to read as much Shakespeare as I do.

"I know. We only have to read The Taming of the

Shrew. And rumor has it then we get to watch Ten Things I Hate About You."

"You're lucky."

"I know. I was always lucky. Even in seventh grade when we did Pygmalion. I was so mad though when we filmed The Hobbit and I didn't get to be Gollum."

"You just want all the attention."

"Shut up. You know you do, too. And actually I really just wanted to get wrapped in plastic wrap."

"You're crazy."

"I know. I used to cry when we read The Little Prince because I was like kids have wisdom. And now every day in English it gets re-enforced. It's like what we say matters."

"What you say always matters to me."

"You're a fabulous liar."

"Maybe. But I love you."

"I love you too."

Chapter 6

Two Months Later

Somehow, by accident. Laurel has ended up alone with four guys in her bedroom. Some of them are on her bed. They are all watching American Pie 2. Laurel had been leaning back against whatever guy was sitting towards the front of the bed with the pillows, but now she plops down next to Jeff. She studies his movements and copies them, trying to get his attention. When that doesn't work, she touches his hand. He doesn't move. Everyone else leaves, and the two of them are left alone.

Laurel whines to Jeff that she does not want him to leave. He was half-expecting something like this, but doesn't show it. He tries to think of ways to comfort her. He touches her arm, but he can tell that she is still hurting. She breathes heavily and reaches her hand up through his shirt to touch his bare chest. He touches her hair and lifts her chin to look up at him. "Look at me. You'll be fine. I promise. You know when I'm gone I'm still in your heart. And you can call me whenever you want, ok?" But her breathing still isn't quite right, so he sits down next to her on her bed.

"I want a hug," she pleads.

"Come here."

They fall back together on her bed, not entirely awkwardly, but not perfectly, but neither of them can find words. She's lying on top of him, trying not to make it sexual. His arms are on her back. His cell vibrates in his jeans pocket. He tries not to move her too much, but sits up and answers it. They look at each other. He's trying to keep her as calm as possible. But he tells her he has to go. She cries out, "No!" He keeps one hand on her side while he picks up one of his sneakers from the floor. She lets moves a little bit to let him know it's ok to let go of her to put his sneakers on, so he does. She stands up while he still sits, tying his sneakers. When he's finished, he stands up and kisses her forehead.

"What are you worried about?" he says. "It's just us. Relax. Nothing's gonna happen, ok?"

She says "ok" and he leaves.

Laurel cries a little. She can't believe he's gone, but she remembers what he said. Even when he's gone, he's still with her, in her heart. After the tears subside, she starts to walk around her house, cleaning it up. She knows it's her responsibility because it was her friends who had been there. As she is cleaning up, she collects the Coke cans, and drinks the remainders of what is in them. She does this because she knows that one of them was Jeff's. His lips were on it, and now hers will be. It doesn't occur to her to save the cans. She tosses them into a recycling bin. She goes upstairs and goes to bed happy.

Chapter 7

One Month Later

Jeff and Laurel are on their cell phones with each other again. Jeff is playing Halo in the background. She is telling him that she is stressed out because of school and that he should help her more with her homework. He does not sound interested in that idea, and says that he has his own homework to do. He continues to play Halo throughout the conversation. It is a Friday and Laurel asks him what he is doing tomorrow.

"Track meet."

"Can I come?"

"You'd be bored."

"But I wanna come."

"No, you don't."

"Can we hang out Sunday?"

"Pats game, baby."

"How 'bout next weekend?"

"I dunno."

"I'm going to a party tonight."

"Will there be a lot of girls?"

"Yes."

"Can I come?"

"We'll see. Actually no. People don't get us. Everyone just thinks you're my boyfriend, and I don't feel like dealing with that."

"I know. You just shouldn't tell people about me."

"It's hard not to. Like what else do us girls have to talk about all day at modeling school? Except I don't talk to the other girls about you, because they're weird and just talk about sex and stuff. But there's this one girl, Kylie, she's a year younger than us, and she's so cute. I love her. And I tell her about you because I think somehow she kind of gets it. And sometimes I need someone to talk to there because it's really busy and I get stressed. Like today we did pilates and it was really hard. And we did commercials, which was more fun than just photo shoots because I hate those. And then we had to do this debate thing about Eminem and it was great because I got to defend him."

"I'm proud."

"So what should I wear tonight?"

"Something sexy."

"So you can call me a whore?"

"Maybe. But you wanna look hot don't you?"

"Yeah. Ok, I'm gonna go. I'll talk to you later, ok?"

"Ok. By the way, it doesn't matter what you wear. You're beautiful."

Chapter 8

A Few Days Later

Laurel was embarrassed, maybe even a little bit ashamed, about what happened at that party. Jeff and Laurel have grown pretty comfortable with each other by now, but she knew that she had a tendency to do stupid things when he wasn't around. He embodied her conscience, plus he seemed to have more common sense than she did. Or at least he was always more rational. But since she always told him everything, she decided she had to tell him this, too. Or so she thought. She picked up her cell to call him.

"Hey. Guess what happened at track practice today? This girl fell so I got to walk her back to the nurse's office and we had this awesome conversation about…"

"Jeff-ey," she says in a way so that he knows something is wrong.

"Uh-oh. What's wrong, baby?"

"I can't tell you."

"Well that's just ridiculous. Come on, what did you do now?"

"Well when you put it that way."

"Ok then fine. Back to my story. So this girl is really cool…"

"It's a boy," she interrupts.

"Look, whatever happened, he's probably a jerk anyway."

"Because he's a guy? That means *you're* a jerk then, too."

"You have a tendency to attract them."

"Like I said…"

"No, I'm just special."

"Yeah, well, I already knew that."

"Look, don't worry about it. There will always be boys. And you'll always have me."

"Yeah, I guess you're right. So anyway I forgot to tell you I switched some of my classes so my grades are getting better. But I don't want to hear you brag about your GPA, ok?"

"Dealio."

"So what are you up to this weekend?"

"I'm supposed to play soccer with some buddies… wanna come?"

"For sure. You can teach me."

"Yeah, right! The only thing you're capable of learning about soccer is how to carry equipment."

"Well, I guess we'll just have to see about that, won't we?"

"Guess so. Later."

Chapter 9

A Few Days Later

Laurel stands in front in a parking lot on the edge of a soccer field when her cell vibrates. She looks out at the field, and up at the sky, taking in the green and blue and beauty. It's sunny and warm but not hot. She's wearing shorts and an oversized tee shirt and holding a water bottle. She looks for Jeff's friends, but sees only him approaching. He tells her she doesn't need her water bottle, although she can't imagine why, but she figures she's not going to waste time debating it so she leaves it by the edge of the grass, at the brown fence. Jeff tells her that she'll have to do without cleats and straps his pads from middle school on her. But he's not in the mood to be nice.

"I take it you're wearing a sports bra...so can you take your shirt off?"

"You're repulsive. I take it you better shut your mouth unless you're wearing a cup."

"Ouch. Got me on that one."

"Can we go now? Aren't your friends down there waiting for us?"

"Um yeah, about that. They left."

"What!"

"The guys had stuff to do."

"Like what? Play video games?"

"Hey, don't insult my Halo. And for your information, I didn't want to go down as cock-blocker of the century. I can't just introduce all my friends to you with me there and no escape. It's obvious you've only got eyes for me

15

when I'm around. Plus, nine guys and one girl? I can't do that to them."

They walk down to the field, where he has goals set up and two giant water bottles.

"You brought me a water bottle. That almost makes up for you lying to me."

"Huh?"

"You idiot. Why did you tell me your friends were coming in the first place?"

"Oh. I changed my mind. And they changed theirs."

"I don't even care. So I get stuck with just you all afternoon?"

"Yup. You can plan on getting dirty, too."

"Ha. Ha."

They play soccer and after a couple of hours, they're both tired and dirty. Not to mention sweaty, not that either of them cares about that when it's just them. As they sit on the green grass, they drink from the water bottles, not looking at each other and not speaking. Eventually, Jeff decides to break the silence. He has a better idea in mind. He punches her shoulder.

"You're pretty good for a beginner."

"Really?"

"No, but I love you anyway."

She laughs, but he keeps his serious tone because he has something else to say. He takes her hand.

"Laurel, I didn't want to tell you this. But I decided I want you in my life. Forever."

"Forever and ever?"

"Well maybe not when I get sick of you," he jokes.

She smiles and says, "Maybe I'll get sick of you first."

They're happy. For the first time, something makes sense to both of them, even if they do not really know what it is. All they know is that they're having a lot of fun. They fake-punch and hit and kick each other until they are practically rolling in the grass. And for a little while, they had forgotten that the rest of the world existed.

Chapter 10

Jeff sits at his piano. Laurel stands next to him, holding lyrics she wrote for him. He plays a note, and she exclaims that it is too loud.

"And since when did you become a musician?"

"I didn't, but it's the wrong feel for the song."

"The song is about us. Half of us is me, so don't I get a say in how it should feel?"

"Jeff, this song is not about your feelings, so get over yourself. If only I could show you."

Jeff pats a spot next to him on the bench and tells her, "Go for it."

"You know I can't play well."

"Well I'm gonna show you so you can show me."

"I'm never gonna be good at this."

"Oh, Laurel. If I can do it, so can you."

"That's what I call twisted logic. But I can see I'm not going to win this one, so show me where to put my fingers."

"Kinky."

"I'll leave."

"Ok, ok. Here."

They work on the song for a while. Neither of them had ever given much thought to emotions being reflected in music, but once their friends hear the song, they get a sense of their feelings for each other. They also know that compromises have been made.

Chapter 11

Laurel has already begun packing for her trip to Florida for April vacation so her bedroom is covered with tiny, brightly-colored tank tops, among other things. It's late on a Thursday night and they have school tomorrow. She's leaving for Florida Saturday morning. She decides it's time to tell Jeff that she won't be around for a week, not that he would necessarily notice. She calls him anyway.

"What are you doing?" she asks.

"Watching the World Poker Tour. How come you're not watching it?"

"Um, because I don't know how to play poker," she replies, annoyed.

"Watch it and you'll learn."

"Why can't you teach me?"

"Because I don't have the patience," he replies, annoyed.

She decides she's not dealing with his mood, so she changes the subject.

"I'm going to Florida for vacation."

"I'll miss you," he says pretending to be cute and dramatic.

"No you won't."

But much to their surprise, he does. So a few days later, he calls her.

"I miss you. I don't want to not talk to you for a week. I don't know how."

"I'm sure you'll figure something out."

"But I have no other girls to talk to every day. Not when we don't have school."

"So go find some girls, Jeff, God. You're handsome enough. I'm confident you can do it."

"Why don't you just admit that you need me too?

"Um, ok, fine. I just don't need you this week. Anyway, why are we fighting? What happened to you?"

"Nothing. I just, I want you in my life forever and ever, remember?"

"Yeah, I remember. Let's do something when I get back, ok? On Sunday?"

"Dealio. Oh my God! Did you see Dane Cook's latest tour?"

"Yeah, I've been watching inappropriate TV when they think I'm sleeping."

"Dane Cook is not inappropriate."

"Well I don't know about that, but the American Pie series sure as hell is and I've been watching that since it's been on."

"Hey, did I tell you about the girl who works in my mom's store? She's got huge boobs."

"You really need to grow up and get over this fascination with boobs. What did you do with her?"

"Oh you have got be kidding me. You can't accuse me of that with her! She's not my type. I just like her boobs."

"Good. The first step is admitting you have a problem. Except that you're not supposed to go around saying that to girls, idiot. It's a miracle I put up with you. And what exactly *is* your type?"

"Ok well you hardly count as female. Yet somehow my type is someone like you."

"But not me?"

"I'm not gonna start a fight."

"You make no sense."

"Don't be mad."

"I'm not. Not at you, anyway. At the universe and why things have to be like this. You just make me sad."

"If I make you so sad, then why do you talk to me?"

"Because no one makes me happier."

"Exactly.

"I love you."

"As long as you mean it how I do, I love you too. Can I tell you a funny story now so you don't go all emotional and cry on me?"

"If you don't want to hear me cry, then hang up."

"No. I'm not going to be responsible for you crying. Especially not for stupid reasons. You're the one making everything complicated."

"I thought you were trying to make me feel better."

"I'm sorry, Laurel, but here's your reality slap for tonight. You over-analyze everything. We have each other the way we are and we're happy. Why do you have to think about the future and crap like that?"

"Jeff, I don't. It's not even the future. But whatever. You're right, as usual. I'm not gonna fight over nothing."

"Can I tell you my story now?"

"You're not gonna let me go to bed until you do, right?"

"Yup."

"Ok Jeff. I'm listening."

Chapter 12

Laurel returned home from Florida on Saturday. She hadn't talked to Jeff for a few days, and she remembered her plans with him for Sunday. She also remembered something else.

"Hey, by the way, what do you want for your birthday?"

"I don't know…a trucker hat!"

"Jeffrey, I am not getting you a trucker hat!"

"You asked me what I wanted."

"Why would you want that?"

"Because I like them. Oh by the way, guess what?"

"Enlighten me."

"I decided I want to be a nerd."

"I'm sorry I must have misheard. I thought you just said you wanted to be a nerd."

"Yeah. Not a geek. Not a dork. Just a nerd. It's so awesome."

"I thought you were trying to attract girls, not repel them."

"Yeah, well, if they don't like it, too bad. This is who I am now."

"A nerd who wears trucker hats? No, I'm pretty sure you're just going through a phase. At least that's what I am going to pray for."

"Speaking of which, I can't see you tomorrow. I forgot I have to go my little cousin's first communion."

"What are you gonna wear?"

"Whatever wrinkled khakis and shirt I find first. Don't worry. You're not missing anything."

Chapter 13

Laurel sits in the middle of a pile of papers, books and binders on her bedroom floor. She wears sweatpants. She feels her cell vibrate because it is sitting to her side, on the floor. She looks stressed and annoyed, especially when Jeff says, "What are you doing?"

"Studying. Why? What are you doing?"

"Not much. Hangin' out."

"Shouldn't you be studying? Finals are in a few days."

"Yeah, well, I'm pretty much good except for that ten page paper for English."

"Ouch. Let's trade. I'll do your English stuff and you can take my math and science finals for me, ok?"

"I'm good."

"Well unfortunately my history final won't be entirely based on everything we were supposed to learn from watching Star Wars. And there's still the debate about the Middle East. I still have to do research. And I actually have to know my English stuff, too. We don't get papers like you. I have to sit and write essays. It sucks. And we can only bring a page of notes for each book we read."

"Poor baby."

"Shut up! I'm gonna go unless you have anything positive to say. Some of us have to study."

"That doesn't sound very positive."

"Well I'm gonna get like 'C's in everything."

"Yeah, that's good, too."

"Well I am."

"No you're not. Haven't I rubbed off on you yet?"

Laurel sighs and says, "Jeff, I need to study, ok?"

"Ok. But I know you're gonna call me before you go to sleep. Don't worry. I'll be waiting."

"Don't."

"Will you relax?"

"Ok but I need to study, Jeff. What is up with you today, anyway?"

"I don't know. I just…I have this feeling about us."

"Like what kind of feeling?

"Like whether or not we like it, we're gonna be stuck with each other forever. Because what could break our bond?"

"I guess you're right."

Chapter 14

Jeff and Laurel are at a house party. At first see they stick close to each other's sides, but then Laurel goes to mingle with other people. Then she goes back to Jeff, who is then sitting on the floor, back against the wall. She sits next to him. They are in a secluded area. The party winds down.

"She wants to me hook up with him."

"Who?"

Laurel points to a boy across the room.

Jeff looks and says, "He's cute. Go for it."

"I don't know why you think this is so funny. So too bad. I'm going to stay here and cock-block you all night."

"That is *not* very nice."

"Now you don't wanna be friends?"

"No, it's just that I would like to meet other girls and your presence is preventing them from coming over here. Most girls aren't as cocky as you and aren't just gonna walk up to a guy when there's a girl with him."

"Why do you need all these other girls?

Jeff looks her over for a good while before finally saying, "Yeah, you're right. You take up pretty much all of my time that could otherwise be spent with other girls anyway."

"That is such a lie! You see them every day at school, and I don't even go to your school so I don't know what you do. And like afterschool, at track practice. You make it seem like hooking up with random people is just fun, but you wouldn't even know, Jeff! But you should know from what I've told you that it's not, ok? It's not!"

Jeff considers this for a moment, and then says, "I know. I'm sorry. And you know I'm not like that. Can you blame me for wanting a girlfriend?"

"Yes! And just to prove it to you, I'm gonna go hook up with that guy!"

Jeff is yearning for her to stay with him. "Laurel, *stop*. You're being stupid. You don't know him. It's not the same as having a boyfriend, ok?"

People walk by holding alcohol and she eyes them.

"Yeah, well you just wanna get drunk. And you know what happens with that? You hook up with random people. So you want to do the same thing that I do anyway without alcohol. You're just as guilty for wanting to be like me. And I don't want you to get drunk, Jeff. That's stupid. I like you how you are."

"You realize you pretty much just called yourself a whore. Anyway, maybe other people will like me better when I'm drunk. Maybe I don't like who I am and I'll like myself better when I'm drunk."

"We can't both have issues right now, ok? Why can't we ever just be happy?"

Jeff seriously thinks about this for a moment. "I don't know. But you can stay here, ok? It's fine."

They both look around and realize that not only is the party winding down, but people are giving them their space, in what was already a secluded area.

Laurel remembers something she wishes she hadn't, but figures she might as well use the opportunity. "Wait. I have to get something. I'll be right back, ok?"

Jeff decides he doesn't need to be anywhere else within the next 30 seconds so he agrees, "I'll be here."

Laurel sits down next to him and hands him a gift bag.

"What's this?"

"Your birthday present."

Jeff opens it, "A trucker hat and chocolate poker chips."

He laughs, and seems truly excited, "Nice. Come here."

He spreads his legs and pats the space in between, gesturing for her to sit there, and she does. While she sits there, he hugs her from behind. She moves a little bit to see his face, and says, "Guess what else?"

"What?"

"Since I decided to embrace whoever you decide to be, while I was on vacation in Maine last week, I got a shirt that says, 'I heart nerds.'"

"Really?"

"Really, really. And someday, someway, you will pay for this."

"Why do you care so much what people think, Laurel? People need to learn to laugh stuff off. It's just a shirt."

"Well this is just a bad night so can we laugh off this night, too?"

"Sure. I mean, if you need to laugh it off, then do it. But everything's fine, ok? But if you don't wanna talk about tonight ever again, then we won't. It's not like it was very eventful anyway."

"I have something else for you."

"What?"

Laurel pulls a piece of paper that are more of her song lyrics out of her pocket and hands it to him, "here."

"You wrote me another love song."

"No. Well I don't know what it is, really."

"I'd be lost without you."

"No. But I would."

"No you wouldn't. You would be just as much of a pain in the ass without me."

"Well yeah, but I'm also a lot braver when you're around."

"It shouldn't be like that, Laurel."

"I know, Jeff-ey. But don't worry. Someday soon God is gonna find a way and make me aware of it."

"You're crazy. God doesn't exist. And how could you know that anyway?"

"I don't know if God exists. But I just know it's going to happen."

"Why would it need to?"

"Because Jeffrey, we can't grow up without it. Things happen and I can't always talk to you when I feel like I need to because you're at soccer or track or whatever."

"So?"

"So someday the universe has to give me a way to cope and feel like you're here when you're not."

"Why do you need me?"

"Why are you so mean?"

"It's an honest question."

"I don't know, Jeff. Why do you need me?"

"I don't."

"Well then I don't need you."

"Well then how come you think someday you'll

feel like I'm with you when I'm not because you need that?"

"I don't know. But since the first day we met I knew you were, like, part of me.'

"Does that mean that you're part of me?"

"I don't know."

"Well why are you more special than me? And how come you get some special way to feel like I'm there when I'm not, but I don't get that for you?"

"I'm definitely not more special than you. Your life is so much better than mine. And as for your other question, I don't know, Jeff. Maybe someday you will."

"Laurel, you know you're some kind of special. But really, I don't have to tell you how special you are to me. And as for your answer, sweetheart, I hope you're right. It would be nice, wouldn't it?"

She leans back so that her head is on his shoulder and he wraps his arms around her and kisses her hair. He moves one hand so that it can link with hers. They look out at whatever is in front of them, not at each other.

Chapter 15

September 2003. Tenth Grade.

The rest of the summer was uneventful. For her fifteenth birthday, he gave her the fifteen-dollar Harley-Davidson keychain she had been wanting and they hung out at the beach. He also bought her a Coke at a local store. She wanted it because it was in a glass bottle and she saved it, because it was from her birthday. They remained as innocent as they had been when they were fourteen. At least for a while. But sooner or later, reality hits all of us. Meanwhile, they were learning a lot from each other. One Friday night they were at a dance together at Laurel's school when she had no problem announcing to him that she has to pee. Trying to pull up her jeans in the bathroom, she noticed a hole in them. After fifteen minutes of waiting outside the girls' room, Jeff decided to walk in and they yell at each other through the stall door.

"Laurel? Are you crying?"

"Oh my God! I can't believe you had the balls to walk into the girls' bathroom!"

"That kind of made no sense. Anyway, I thought you hung yourself or something. But I can't help you with your womanly issues so can we please go now?"

"I can't!"

"Well I can't deal with this."

"Just take off your pants and put them over the stall door...or else I take back what I said about you having balls."

"At the moment I wish I didn't…at least not in the metaphorical sense. Why do you need my pants?"

"Because there's a hole in the crotch of mine and it's too big to just walk out like this. And since we both decided to be stupid tonight and not bring jackets or sweatshirts, what else am I gonna do?"

"Well, what am I supposed to do? Wear *your* pants?"

"You have boxers. I'm not walking out in front of all those people I have to go school with every day in my underwear. It's teeny. And I'm not giving you any more details!"

Jeff laughs and says, "Oh man. I'm glad we know each other's underwear preferences."

"This isn't funny."

"Yes it is and stop crying. You're such a baby. At least now I know not to go anywhere with you without an extra pair of shorts."

He takes off jeans and puts them over stall door.

"Fine you can take my pants. I will proudly walk out of here in my boxers…just as long as we walk fast. My mom should be outside by now anyway."

She opens the stall door, wearing his pants and holding hers. She takes a step out, towards him, and gives him a pouty face with her lower lip.

Jeff kisses her cheek and says, "Adorable." Laurel smiles, takes his hand, and says, "Let's go." They walk out, and she realizes that the world has not come to an end. In fact, nobody even really noticed.

Chapter 16

Laurel had a bit of excitement at school today. She feels the need to talk to Jeff. As soon as she thinks soccer practice is over, she calls him. He doesn't answer, so she tries to distract herself with MTV. And then she calls him again.

"You didn't answer your phone before."

"I just got home from soccer practice like half an hour ago and I was trying to get some stuff done before I knew you'd call me again."

She sarcastically says, "Thanks!"

"What's wrong, Laurel?"

"Nothing."

Jeff tries to cheer her up by saying something that makes her laugh, but eventually has to go back to saying, "tell me what's wrong."

When Laurel doesn't respond, he says, "I love you. Now tell me what's wrong."

"Well since we were outside in the woods for Wellness class, and of course I felt all the pressure to volunteer again, so I did. Anyway, I was walking to history class, but I took my time because we've been just watching Pleasantville, and I caught a glimpse of this like freckle thing under my belly button, and I was like whatever, because I thought it was just a freckle. Then I went in the bathroom and accidentally felt the thing and I was like holy crap! Because there was a tick on me! And I like almost cried for like a second and then I hyperventilated all the way to the nurse's office. And then she was stupid and threw it away, but I guess she knew it wasn't a deer tick."

"Cool. I never had a tick on me."

"Jeffrey!"

"What-ey?" He pauses for a moment, then, "You're fine, Laurel. You had a more exciting day than me, ok? That's all. Relax."

"Ok but English class is killing me. I don't get what's so great about The Great Gatsby."

"Stop complaining."

"Why?"

"Because, Laurel. You have nothing real to complain about. And I'm not saying I do, either, but that's why you don't see me complaining, ok?"

"I want to get good grades in English. It's not my fault I got stuck in a crappy class with a crappy teacher reading boring books so all I can do is stick the silver part of gum wrappers to my binder and write stuff for you. I wish I could draw better, because that would be something else to do, but I never know what to draw."

"How do you know what to write? To me, I mean."

"I don't know...I just do. I kind of just write down words in my head that come to me when I think about you. It's natural, I guess."

"Why don't you just take notes?"

"I don't need to. I'm getting them from the guy who sits next to me."

"Ooh!"

"No, it's not like that. He's like you."

"Except I'm better."

"Well, yeah, actually, that's true. And you're both pretty damn full of yourselves."

"Aren't you getting decent grades on your papers about The Great Gatsby anyway?"

"Yeah."

"Ok so what are you whining about? You get other people's notes for the info for your papers, and you get good grades on them no matter what because you can write."

"It doesn't mean I don't have to think of ideas. And as far as I'm concerned, I'm working with boring material. I mean, I could write a book about us and it would be more interesting than the guy's relationship with the woman."

"Yeah, well, interesting is one description and love story is another. What you're reading is a love story."

"So? I could write something about us that could be an interesting non-love story."

"You're so crazy. Nobody cares about complications. That's why people write fiction. Because it's pretty. And you can make up love stories."

"Well I'm not writing fiction and I'm not making up love stories. Someday I will prove to you that people will care about us. And in case you haven't noticed, they already do. I get questioned about us on a daily basis because people don't get it. Don't you think they'll want to know?"

"We'll see. Besides, what would you tell them?"

"What *should* I tell them?"

"Tell them we're too young to know."

"Years from now, we won't be so young."

"Laurel, I don't think we'll ever know how to accurately explain ourselves to the world. Because I don't think even the two of us will ever understand it. You should just stop telling people about me."

"I try, Jeff. I try so hard. But I don't want to have to hide it from the world, because you make me so happy. And sometimes I talk about it to see if we're the only ones or if there are people who can give me advice."

"How could you possibly need advice about anything about me?"

"We fight a lot."

"Because of you."

"This is exactly what I mean."

"Well I tell you when you're being stupid or just plain bitchy. So why don't you tell me when I'm being a jerk?"

"I don't know. Because I can't. Because you're not perfect but you're better than me so who am I to tell you when you're wrong? And because it hurts me, Jeff. I can't insult you like that."

"First of all you're not better than me. You're just being stupid again. And you should either start calling me a jerk or not let me tell you when you're being a bitch. If you can't be honest with me, then this is dumb. And technically that would mean I can't trust you."

"But I trust you more than anyone."

"I know you do. That's why I'm always trying to help you and teach you things. So here's your lesson of the day. Stop loving me so much and tell me I'm a jerk."

"You *are* a jerk. Sometimes."

"Good. Was that so hard?

"No."

"Hey, I got something for you."

"What?"

"Hold on. I gotta put the phone down; I'll be right back, ok?"

"Ok." She hears him sing her lyrics and play piano over the phone. "Jeff-ey."

"What-ey?"

"I love the beginning and I like the middle part. The end needs a little something more to it."

"I'm glad you like it. It's for you. I'll work on it."

"You finally decided I'm worth something?"

"If you aren't worth anything, I wasted a lot of effort on you already."

"Naw, you just got nothing better to do but write me love songs."

"And you just got nothing better to do than write me letters in English class."

"Yeah, but that's because it's class. What else am I supposed to do?" There is a pause, and then she says, "Let's just call it even, ok?"

"Good. Homework time?"

"Homework time."

"Call me before you go to sleep?"

"Yeah, because you stay up till two every day and I don't know how."

"I'm gifted."

"Some of us need beauty sleep."

"Not you."

"Um, thanks, I think."

"You're welcome."

"Ok I'll call you tonight."

"K."

Chapter 17

Jeff and Laurel are at a house party. Laurel has fallen in love with another boy named Jake. She hasn't told Jeff yet, but since now she's convinced that Jake is going to stick around longer than to be just another of her flavors of the week, whatever that means when you're fifteen and innocent, she figures it's time to tell Jeff.

"I've been waiting to tell you something."

"Is it about a guy?"

"Maybe."

"There are other people around, ya know."

"You're such a perv!"

"Ok. His name is Jake. I'm in love with him. Everything about him is perfect."

"Is everything about me perfect?"

"No."

"Wanna know why?"

"Not really, but get on with it."

"It's because you see yourself in me, and that includes everything you don't like about yourself. All your flaws are mine, too."

"I wouldn't go that far."

"Fine. But I bet you anything this guy doesn't remind you of yourself like I do. I bet he looks nothing like me, and meanwhile you think if you were a guy you'd have my amazing body."

"You're right. He doesn't look like you. But your ears are way more adorable if you really want to know."

"Look, anyway, you're not in love with this guy. Trust me."

"I trust that you don't know anything about this."

"You and I are not even fifteen and a half years old."

"What the hell is your point? If there were any rules about these things, it's not like you're the expert anyway. And for the record, he's our age too."

"Yeah, and for the record, do you realize how dangerous guys our age are? Do you even know what we talk about when girls aren't listening?"

"Probably football. And by the way, Jake plays baseball. And he isn't a jerk like you. And he's innocent and sweet."

"Maybe he is, but nobody is perfect, ok?"

"Ok fine. But there has never been a time when I've been with him that I've ever really thought about anything else."

"So what? If I allowed it, you would be that way with me all the time, too."

"Yeah, but I'm not in love with you. It's different. I only act that way with you because..."

"Because why?"

"You know I love you."

"Yup, so what's the big deal?"

"I just, I feel like I have to pay attention to you when you're with me, because if I don't maybe someday you'll leave."

"Why would you say that?"

"I don't know. Because maybe you're only using me for attention."

"Now there's an interesting theory. Look, if anyone's leaving, you're going to leave me for Jake."

"No I won't."

"So what if you ever marry him? What are you gonna do about me then?"

"Then you'll still be my best friend. He already knows, Jeff," she says as she takes his hand.

"I wanna meet him," he says as he stares into her eyes.

"I don't want you to meet him," she says and let go of his hand.

"Why not?"

"Because he's not like you, ok?"

"How can you be in love with someone who's not like me?

"Stop flattering yourself! Jeff, just leave it alone, ok?"

"Ok. Come here."

He pulled her to him and held her, believing that he had won. To be sure, he kissed her cheek to see if he would get one back. He did.

"I don't wanna fight about Jake. I'm always gonna want you, ok?"

Jeff still holds her hips, and she still loosely holds his arms. He says, "Shh. I know. It's ok. Tell me something. What's it like?"

"What's what like?"

"Being in love."

"Well, with you I'm just me. But with Jake, I'm nervous. It makes me want to puke. But in a good way."

"Weird."

Even though they had been talking about a romantic kind of love, they weren't thinking about it. Because in this moment, all they knew for sure was that they had each other. And that's all they thought about.

Chapter 18

Jeff and Laurel are on their cell phones with each other again. They're fighting because Jeff wants to watch Family Guy instead of talk to her.

"South Park is so much better anyway. And you're being stupid."

"What is your problem tonight?"

"Nothing."

"Exactly. I don't have to fix anything with you right now so can I please catch this break and go enjoy my show? Why don't you go call Jake?"

"He's writing a zillion page paper. He works a lot harder than you do."

"Shut up. I'm leaving."

"Good."

"Laurel."

"*What!*"

"You can call me after."

"Maybe I don't want to."

"I don't know why you try to lie to me when I can read your mind."

"Well stop using it to your advantage."

"Only if you promise me you'll chill out."

"Ok. I'm fine. I'll talk to you later.

"Ok. Bye."

"Bye."

They flip their cells shut, and she does call him back later, partially because she can't think of anything better to do. The next day, he calls her and she tells him that she can only talk for a few minutes, "because Jake is gonna call me so we can watch Newlyweds."

He starts to crack up.

"Wait. Are you trying to tell me you guys watch TV together over the phone? That's the lamest thing I ever heard!"

"Next time I want your opinion, I'll ask for it. And who are you to talk? You don't have a girlfriend."

"I don't have a girlfriend because the single life is better. And Jake's not your boyfriend, which by the way, means he's not in love with you."

"No, Jeff. It means he understands we're young and we don't need to make a commitment yet. And *your* single life is definitely not better so don't even go there."

"You really should stop hooking up with other guys. One day Jake won't be able to handle it anymore."

"You don't even know him."

"Well is he getting other girls?"

"Well, no. I don't think so."

"And you think it's ok that you can do whatever you want? If the guy's in love with you, you two have some problems to work out."

"Because *you* would know anything about any of this."

"Hey, I've been hanging out with girls, ok?"

"What girls?"

"From track."

"Whatever. Doesn't make you an expert. Jake and I have engagement rings anyway."

"Did you just say what I think you just said?"

"Why?"

"*Why*? You two can't decide to be an official couple,

but you have engagement rings? Tell me how that makes sense."

"I don't have to tell you anything. And I have to go."

"Why? Because I'm gonna make him jealous?"

"He has nothing to be jealous of. He cares about me more than you do."

"Don't ever say that."

"Well then stop acting like a jerk."

"Fine. But usually I do it *because* I care."

"Whatever, Jeff. Can I go now?"

"You know you love me."

"You just want attention. I think you're jealous of Jake."

"Not exactly. But I like your attention, so can I get some?"

"Jeff, you know I love you."

"Good girl. I suppose you can go and enjoy your boy toy now."

"Yeah, ok. Bye!"

"Bye, babe."

They flip their cells shut. Laurel thinks for a moment before calling Jake back.

"Hey, I kept calling you."

"I know, I know. Jeff wouldn't leave me alone. Sorry."

"Is he bothering you again? Because he shouldn't insult you. That's not what best friends do."

"No, it's..."

"Is everything ok?"

"Yeah. Everything's great, Jake, ok? I promise."

Chapter 19

Jeff's cell vibrates and he answers it. He's distracted and unhappy because he's grounded. Again. But since it's Laurel and he can't think of anything better to do, he answers it. He gives her a "what's up?" but she knows him all too well, and says, sarcastically, "you sound awfully happy to talk to me."

"No, it's, it's not you. I'm grounded again."

"You're always grounded."

He doesn't say anything, so she says, "I'm sorry. It's too bad. I was gonna ask you to hang out tonight because Jake apparently has other plans."

Jeff is so intrigued by this fact that he sounds excited.

"Really?"

"Don't make that into something it's not, ok? He had to do something. Unlike you, who routinely blows me off for the guys."

"Well I can't see them when I'm with you, so when I am supposed to hang out with them?"

"You see them every day at school and some of them at practice."

"It's not the same."

"Ok. Fair enough."

"So what are you gonna do tonight?"

"Probably just hang at Kaylie's. You?"

"Honestly...play Halo till I fall asleep.

Laurel recalls an episode of Laguna Beach and decides to use the same words Jessica does and attempt her best voice for it and see if it works.

"Are you lying?"

"Well now that you've shaken it out of me, I've actually been working on one of your songs."

"You just said *honestly* you're gonna play Halo."

"I just left out that song part. It's not like I was lying. I just wanted it to be a surprise."

"Aw."

"Awwwww."

"Ok I'm gonna go call Kaylie. I'll call you later tonight if I can."

"K."

A few days later, Laurel's cell vibrates. She was annoyed at Jeff for not answering his phone when she actually did call when she was with Kaylie. And after that she hasn't tried to call him. But he hasn't tried to call her until now.

"Jeff," she says in her annoyed voice.

"I know you're mad. Let's go running tomorrow. Just the two of us, baby."

"No, you'll get your practice in. You're just pretending to do this for me."

"Have I *pretended* anything for you before?"

"How should I know? I just know you can run a lot faster."

"First of all I've never really deceived you and I don't plan to."

Laurel morphs back into Jessica just to make sure he's behaving.

"You swear?"

"Yup."

"Swear on our relationship?"

Jeff says, half-sarcastically, "Of course, darling.

Anyway, I promise I'll keep you at my side tomorrow. Ok?"

"K."

Chapter 20

Laurel is asleep under her purple covers. It's Sunday and not yet ten. She suddenly awakens because she feels her cell vibrate next to her pillow. She looks at the clock then looks at her cell to see who it is and answers it with the intention of keeping him quiet.

"It's ten in the morning. On Sunday. Either you're trying to kill me or you're asking for it."

"Give it to me, baby."

"*Why are you calling me!*"

Jeff remains chipper, but because he's him, can't resist playing with her. Even if it is ten in the morning on a Sunday.

"*Because!* We're going running."

"I'm sleeping."

"Ok but you better be at the track in an hour and a half."

"Or else what?"

"Or else I really am better than you. And maybe I'll leave your life forever."

"Jeffrey Mark!"

"Take a joke, Laurel Ann! But really, you better be there."

He flips his cell shut. She turns hers off, knowing that she won't be able to go back to sleep now but there's nobody else she needs to talk to. After screaming into her pillow, she looks in her drawers for warm running clothes. Jeff sits on the track, stretching. Today, he wants to make her work, at more than just running. He's been trying to convince himself that he's more interested in himself than he is in Laurel, because after all, they're only friends, but he hasn't been able to shake the need to prove something to himself. He just does a fantastic job of hiding it. He sees her approach and pretends not to notice until she's standing over him.

"Can I step on your crotch now?"

He covers his crotch.

"Nope. You can stand there all day or we can get on with this."

When she sits down next to him, he says, "Put your arm like this, yeah. Good."

They stretch in silence for a few minutes. Then he stands up and offers her his hand but she won't take it and stands up on her own.

"So where's Jake today?"

"How should I know?" she responds and starts to walk. He follows.

"I don't know. I thought you knew these things."

"Not exactly. He's been kind of distant lately."

"Trouble in paradise? Can I say I told you so yet?"

"No! And there's no trouble. It's just, I don't think I know him as well as I thought I did. I don't know him like I know you."

"You don't know everything about me."

"Well maybe you don't know everything about me."

Jeff laughs, "You're only kidding yourself. I think I know you better than *you* do."

They run, and when Jeff realizes she's not going to talk to him until he changes the subject, he does that. He hugs her good-bye, but it is quick. She seems very distracted. Six days later, she calls him, crying. He answers and all she can say is "Jeff." He knows that something is very wrong, and for once turns off the TV to listen to her.

Chapter 21

"What's wrong?"

"It's Jake. I didn't talk to you last week because of midterms, but Jake and I did talk and I thought that everything was ok but this week I haven't talked to him at all and I keep leaving these voicemails but I don't know what to say and he's not calling me back and that's so unlike him and what is going on!"

"Slow down. He might just need some time, ok? Did you guys have a fight?"

"No. No. I don't know what happened. Everything was fine and now I don't think he's gonna talk to me like ever again and what did I do, Jeff? What did I do?"

"Shh. You didn't do anything. It's not your fault. He's a jerk."

"No! No! You don't get it! He's not like that."

"Listen to me. I'm a guy, ok? I know how guys are. Just because they seem nice, doesn't mean they're not capable of doing bad things."

"He can't just leave without saying good-bye."

"Laurel. He's a jerk. Think about it. He was being selfish and didn't want to deal with saying good-bye to you."

"I don't get how he could do this."

"I know you don't. I know. It's not your fault. Let's go running tomorrow and talk about it, ok?"

"Are you *crazy*? I can't go *running*. I don't think I can *move*. I want to puke. I want to lie on my floor and bleed to death. And I'm never leaving my room again!"

"Laurel, you're fifteen. Don't be ridiculous."

"I know! Things like this don't happen to people our age! I'm too young to deal with this!"

"Well dealing with it like a twelve year-old isn't going to solve anything. I promise it will get easier."

"Oh, because *you* would know. What am I supposed to do, Jeff?"

"You have so much ahead of you. And I know you can't see it right now, so hang out with me tomorrow."

"No! I don't trust boys anymore and I'm going to hate all of them, starting with you."

"Will you be rational for once? You can't hate me just because I was born the opposite of you. I didn't ask for that."

Laurel is crying and she yells at him, "Well I didn't ask for God to put you in my life, ok?"

"Jesus Christ, Laurel! What is *wrong*?"

"Jake and I were in love with each other. And you and I aren't. What do we have that's going to keep us together forever? One day you're gonna leave, too. I'm not stupid, Jeff!"

"Ok so *that's* what this is about. Honey, I have been in your life. And you have been in mine. Practically every day for like two years. And we love each other, remember? Calm down."

"Well Jake and I loved each other and it wasn't enough for us."

"Ok, but unlike him, I'm not hiding parts of myself from you. And when you're being a pain in the ass, I tell you. I believe he was in love with you, I do, but sometimes that's not enough. If he didn't feel like he could tell you all his other feelings about you, it wasn't gonna last anyway."

Laurel says, sarcastically, "Thanks. That really helps."

"I told you. It's not your fault. And he's a jerk. I don't know how someone could ever do something like that to you. You're too precious. I promise you'll be ok and I'll be here. And you know what you should tell him if he ever *does* call you again?

Laurel is a little happier now, and interested to see what he will say.

"What?"

Jeff had been busy finding Michael Jackson's Beat It! He turns up the volume at the right part, so she hears, 'beat it!' She laughs and he knows this is as good as it's gonna get for now, but he also knows it's all he can do.

Chapter 22

Jeff is at a house party. He's talking college basketball with his buddies. They hadn't gotten to the point of chatting up the girls yet. But as soon as he walked in, Jeff put his and Laurel's names on the beer pong waiting list. He knows the only girl he'll really get to talk to tonight is her, and that's ok with him, especially because people seem to think that they look pretty good together. He turns and sees her, and knows that he has to act as bubbly as some of the girls there.

"Come here, you!"

He hugs her. She's still not happy and does not want to accept the fact that she is at a party, so she keeps one hand on his back so that his friends won't really notice. She doesn't want attention from anyone but him right now.

He looks into her eyes and quietly says, "What's wrong, baby girl?"

"I don't wanna be here" she whispers to the side of his face.

His friends move away from them a few feet. He no longer cares what they do tonight. He smiles at her and says, "You're a horrible liar." He knows she'll understand and is slightly amused.

"Yeah, I guess you haven't taught me well enough yet. But it's so wrong, Jeff!"

"What have *you* been smoking?"

"Because of Jake. I'm out having fun. Which probably why he left in the first place. I shouldn't be having fun without him."

Jeff knows that there are approximately three ways

to deal with that. It doesn't take him more than three seconds to choose one.

"Well you better get used to it, because I don't think he's coming back, and I can't have a best friend who doesn't know how to party."

He knows he chose the right one when she let go of him.

"You're not funny."

"Really?"

"Really."

"Well maybe you're right. But it just so happens I got our names bumped up on the ruit list before you even got here and we're next. And don't worry, we're not playing with booze. So you can sit there all night, alone, since I know you're not gonna talk to guys tonight, or you can come play with me. In fact, I challenge you to beat me."

"That's so not fair! You know I can't refuse that game...or an opportunity to kick your butt!"

"Nobody said life was fair."

"I hate you!"

"You love me."

"Yeah...I do."

Jeff kisses her somewhere and says, "Come on. Let's go have fun."

And that was that. Two teenagers exposed to too much of the world at too young of an age. Fortunately for them and those who cared about them, one had a good head on his shoulders and always knew exactly what to do. The other, well, it's a good thing she had him. But she was already changed, and the worst was yet to come. What Jake had done had a lasting impact, and Jeff would soon learn that there was only so much he could do.

Chapter 23

Sometime during the first week of April her sophomore year of high school, Laurel was still devastated. She cried over Jake every night, and kept wondering what had happened. She could not focus on anything, especially not school. Life seemed like a blur, or maybe more like a tornado, and Jeff was just there, because he was always just there. They talked every day, but it didn't really make a difference…at least that's what she thought at the time. Meanwhile, she wasn't in the mood for his antics, even if she had been pulling a few of her own.

"Guess what I did for April Fool's Day."

"No."

"You *love* April Fool's Day. Still not over Jake, huh?"

"Yeah."

"Ok so guess what I did."

"I don't think I could if I tried."

"Well we all had this biology test today, but none of us have been paying attention in class lately. And the test was supposed to be really hard. So we were all studying together a couple days ago, and then we decided to write each other's names on our tests instead of our own, and we drew the most ridiculous pictures, too. Because we figured we're all gonna get about the same grade anyway, so why not just draw pictures that now we can't get in trouble for?"

"Um, doesn't the teacher like know your handwriting?"

"Yeah but he's cool. He wouldn't take the time to figure it out."

"If you put half the effort into school that you do into planning stuff like that..."

"Oh be quiet. I'm not the one who can't take a math test without drawing cartoons on it."

"*You* be quiet. My teachers appreciate my art."

"Do they appreciate my name with hearts around it?"

"I don't know, but you do."

"Yeah. So...do you think you're ready to go running yet?"

"I don't know. It's been so long."

"That's why we should do it."

"Why can't I do it by myself?"

"Because I know you won't unless I get you started. You need a motivation."

Laurel laughs to him, "And *you're* supposed to be my motivation? Oh, that's great."

"Look, I know you're too embarrassed to do it with anyone else who actually runs on a daily basis. So unless you have any better ideas, you should admit defeat now."

Laurel jokingly says, "Never!"

"You're funny. I have this thing with a friend tonight. You gonna be ok?"

"If I knew that wasn't code for something really stupid and boyish, I would say, ooh, how mysterious."

"Laurel."

"What?"

"Are you gonna be ok?"

"It depends what you mean by ok."

"Ok I'm gonna fix that now. I love you."

"Aww."

"Awwwww."

"I love you too. Go have fun."

"K. I'll talk to you later."

"Wait!"

"What?"

"You're right. I *do* love April's Fool's Day, and I couldn't resist doing *something* to get me in a little trouble at school…so in Biology, History, and Spanish, I intentionally fell off my chair."

"Did you get in trouble?"

"No. I mean I couldn't because the senior boys do it like every day, but I figured it was less risky on April's Fool's Day. Besides, what kind of trouble could I possibly be in at my school? They don't give detentions for *that*."

"Yeah, but you cry every time you have to talk to a teacher you don't *love* alone."

"Not true!"

"I mean if you're in trouble."

"Ok enough already. I took some kind of risk, didn't I?"

"Yeah, I know you're not exactly thrilled about your educators this year."

"Fancy. Getting an early start on PSAT studying, or do you just like showing off to me?"

"Oh please. You know you're better in English."

"Not this year."

"You don't know that. You just know I'm not telling you my English grades this year."

"Yeah, and I know *why*."

"Don't make assumptions. Anyway, I'm proud of you for what you did today. Maybe right now you can only take baby steps, but we're going running tomorrow and I'm gonna help you with your stride."

"I'm not digging the irony or the metaphors at the moment."

"See you tomorrow?"

"Fine."

"Bye, baby."

She hangs up. She's not interested in much of anything he says these days. She doesn't care. She figures he's just a stupid boy. And she can't focus. The next day at the track, she tells him that she does not want to be there. But he tries his best for her.

"I know you don't wanna be here, but it's good for you."

"I feel like crap."

"Which is another reason you're here."

"I mean, physically, too. I don't think I have the strength to run."

"You really need to get over this whole Jake thing."

"Believe me, I would if I knew how. It kind of makes me too sad to eat. But it's not just him. It's like when I had bronchitis a few weeks ago, I developed this gag reflex that hasn't gone away yet, and it's like I'll take a few bites and then want to puke."

Jeff is shocked and concerned. "But you don't, right?"

"No, because thank God I hate puking. But really, it's like, it's just hard, ok? Anyway it's not such a bad thing because I'll lose weight and not look fat."

Now he is really mad. "Laurel Ann! Are you insane?"

"No, why?"

"Because. *You* are *not* fat, ok?

"Ok whatever."

Jeff is still mad. "*No*, not whatever. You're like a size zero and with everything else you're feeling right now, fat shouldn't be one of them. I can only help you with so much at a time. You're really crazy to think that, anyway."

"*Ok fine*. I'm gonna start criticizing *you* if you don't leave me alone."

"That's fine because unlike *you*, I can take it."

"You think you're helping?"

"Yeah, I do."

"Then tell me how I am supposed to move on like everyone keeps saying, because I don't know how, Jeff!"

He takes a softer tone.

"Oh, Laurel. I wish I knew. But you have to figure it out for yourself."

"You can only say that because you've never been in this position. You have no *idea* what it feels like."

"You're right I don't. So why don't we both admit we're fifteen and we know nothing about love."

"How can you say that?"

"Because what you had with Jake couldn't have lasted in the real world. Think about if we were older and you guys went to the same college or something. You can't just have perfection forever. People who are in love fight, Laurel. It's normal. And you and Jake didn't fight. Because he never told you anything important. What he did to you was messed up in the first place."

"Oh that's great, Jeff. That really makes me feel spectacular."

"The truth hurts, babe. But you know what?"

"What?"

"Maybe we don't know how everything is supposed to work in any kind of relationship, since I haven't had a girlfriend in years and maybe you just attract guys who don't know how to treat you, but we have each other. And we love each other. And we always will. We can't predict the future, and I definitely don't know how to make everything perfect for you. All we can really do is appreciate what we have. And I miss you. Now you just cry all the time over a guy who's not worth it. He doesn't deserve your tears, Laurel. I know you think he does, but I have a feeling that one day when we're older, you'll see it my way. I want the old version of you back. I want you to not care what people think, and I want you to be fearless again, because you're more fun to hang out with that way, but also because it's better for you. You're wrong to become self-conscious just because of Jake. You just get ideas in your head about things he didn't like about you, which probably aren't true, anyway. I just want you to be you. You're like so scared of the world now, and you never used to be that way."

"I just don't want to get hurt again."

"I know. I don't want you to, either. But you can't just be like this forever. And it will get better. And luckily you have me to complain to when the world is scary."

"What if you're scary?"

Jeff can't keep from laughing. "Are you *really* that worried about what I would ever to you?"

"No, I'm pretty sure you're stuck with me forever."

"I'm pretty sure you're right. Now let's go. If you catch me, I promise not to get a girlfriend and to focus all of my attention on you instead until I at least meet a girl who will go out with me."

"How does that even make sense?"

He starts running and yells back, "Because I'll stop hitting on your friends. Now let's go!"

She runs after him.

"Hey, wait! Jeff! That's not fair!"

Plenty of things in life are unexpected and unfair. All we can do is make the best of them, but Jeff made them funny when he could, and all she could do was try to catch up to him. Which in the end, was in fact good for her. Just like he said.

Chapter 24

Jeff and Laurel are at a house party that is getting more lame by the minute. They're sitting next to each other with their backs against the wall. Jeff points at a girl who walks by.

"She's got a nice rack. What's her name?"

"I can't believe I'm missing the Red Sox game for this. And like I'm really telling you."

"Not my fault you weren't fast enough."

"You know that wasn't fair. I hadn't run in months."

"No problem. I'll go ask her myself."

"You're such a dick."

Jeff smiles and says, "I just wanted to see your reaction."

"Yeah, um, my point exactly."

"You're cute when you're mad. I can't help it."

Laurel is completely unfazed by his whole attitude and sarcastic tone tonight. She's used to it now and it doesn't bother her anymore. And she remembers, "I have something for you. After finals I got really bored and finally decided I had to go out in public again."

"Congratulations, but where is this going?"

"Anyway, I went to the mall, and, here."

She pulls out a small gift bag from behind her back.

Jeff opens it.

"Boxers."

"You know, now that we know each other's underwear preferences and all."

"How intimate. I have something for you, too actually."

"Please don't tell me you got me the female equivalent of…"

Jeff interrupts her by reaching into his pocket and pulling out two friendship bracelets and putting one on his wrist and one on hers.

"What are these for?"

"I know you've been through a lot and I know you're scared. So these are for forever, Laurel. I'm not going anywhere. I wouldn't want to live without you."

Laurel is pretty shocked that all of this is coming from him. She looks at the bracelet on her wrist, then looks back at him, and says, quietly, "Oh my God, Jeff-ey."

Jeff looks right at her and says, "Laurel-ey, I love you."

"I love you, too."

They hug. They have completely forgotten that there are other people around, and when they notice people staring at them, as people always did, but this was exceptional, they just laughed.

Chapter 25

Jeff and Laurel sit next to each other in a movie theater. They're watching the credits at the end of Catwoman.

"Thanks for coming to see Halle Berry with me."

"I thought you wanted to see this because it was about Catwoman."

"Well, Halle Berry is hot. Maybe you should turn bi or something. Then you could appreciate the sexiness of it."

"Maybe you should turn gay or something. Then you could appreciate it every time I say a guy is hot."

"Nah, I'm good."

"Yeah, me too. But for the record you got nothin' on Matt Damon."

"And for the record you got nothin' on Kate Beckinsale."

Jeff takes her hand as they walk out. Once they're outside, she pulls her hand back to her.

"What was that for?"

"I know I can't give you everything you want. I know we'll probably never be in love with each other. I know I'm not Jake. I know we hate each other as much as we love each other. But I need to stop being so mean to you."

"Um…ok…what does that have to do with the whole hand-holding thing?"

"I figure it's all I can do for now. Without making everything between us more confusing. You don't need that now, and I don't want to ruin our friendship."

"Oh please. Like *that* would ever happen."

"All I know is that years from now, you're going to wish I was there. And it's going to get harder to be there for you all the time."

"I'm glad you think our relationship is based on my supposed inability to cope with life without you."

"I didn't say that. And that's not what I mean, either. But it's just, we don't know what could happen, ok? As of right now, we really don't know how to be teenagers without each other."

"And you're saying that I'll never know how to live without you?"

"No, actually I'm quite confident you'll figure that one out. I guess what I'm really saying is that we're in this life and on this planet together. Holding your hand means that we're going to fight. We're going to drag each other through Hell if we have to. It's what we do best. But it also means that whatever we experience, we do it together. So yeah, maybe once I get to college I'm gonna join a frat and drink and smoke weed all the time and maybe you won't do any of that and you're gonna give me Hell for some of it, but I *will* share my experiences with you. Even if we go to different schools. We're gonna be part of each other's lives forever, and I'm not gonna let you miss a beat. Because that's what you do with me, even when I have to shake stuff out of you and make you cry, and you deserve that back from me. I suddenly realized how important it is because I miss you when I don't have it. You've changed since Jake, you know, but you've never been afraid of anything with me. I don't want to have to miss you. I don't want to have to leave."

"Why would you have to leave?"

"I'm not saying I'm planning on going anywhere, but I just want you to know that I'll never let go of your hand, ok? If you let go, Laurel, if you let me out of your heart, don't be mad at me Don't make it my fault. I'll always be holding your hand. I'll always be in your heart, and if you ever need advice, just do what you always do and think of what I would do."

Laurel becomes scared and sad.

"Why are we having this conversation?"

"Because I'm sixteen and you will be soon. I feel like we're getting older. You've been in love. You've been through a lot. But everyone knows you're young to have been through all that, even though some of it was your fault."

"Thanks?"

"No, listen. It makes me think that once I'm older, I'm gonna do everything you've already done, probably plus a lot more that you wouldn't approve of. And I don't want you to get mad at me."

"Jeff, how am I supposed to know what I will or won't be mad at you for years from now?"

"Well first of all if I had to guess, I would say it's probably the exact same stuff you'd be mad at me for if I did it tomorrow. And I just feel like things are going to change, but I just want you to know that no matter what, I'm always holding your hand, ok?"

Laurel takes his hand.

"Ok....Hey you know that party we went to last year?"

"Yeah, why?"

"Well, remember how I said that God is gonna have to give me a way to cope when you're not around, like how I'll be able to feel like you're with me even if when you're not?"

Jeff thinks about it for a moment, and then understands.

"Yeah, you're exactly right. I already know how you've already started feeling, because you've told me. It's like it all came true, didn't it?"

Jeff has shocked himself with his own words.

"It's like a miracle, Jeff-ey."

"Maybe it is. You think it'll work for me, too? Like I'll feel like you're with me even when you're not?"

Laurel looks up at him.

"Definitely. You'll probably think about me even when you don't want to. But you don't think this means that something bad is going to happen to us, though, right? Like you don't think that just because we have something, well actually all kinds of things, that most people don't, that God has to pull us away from each other, because it's like too good to be true?"

"Us? Too good to be true?"

Jeff cracks up at ridiculousness of that idea.

"Well, yeah, ok."

"Besides, we're gonna be stuck with each other forever whether we like it or not."

"I know. And I believe you. I'm just not so sure what stuck with each other means or what forever means. Because if we can feel like we're with each other when we're not, then we are stuck with each other in a way. And is forever limited to this life?"

"Ok *this* conversation is over, babe. I have an idea."

"Now *there's* a scary concept."

"Let's sing."

"Um, no."

"Come on! It's fun. And I'm making it my current mission in life to make you fearless. Besides, no one's gonna hear you except me, and I'm pretty sure we're not afraid of embarrassing ourselves in front of each other anymore."

"That really depends on the level of embarrassment."

"Ok I walked out of your school in front of girls in my boxers. Let's go."

"I am so gonna kill you."

"You are *so* gonna put that energy into your voice."

"Fine. But we're singing Don't Stop Believin by Journey."

"Ok fine you win. Let's just sing."

If Jeff's mission in life actually had been to make her fearless, especially without him around, he hadn't succeeded yet. He never would. But in that moment, he was one step closer. They sang until they couldn't sing anymore because they couldn't stop laughing. They felt like children.

Chapter 26

Laurel is in her bedroom getting ready for her sixteenth birthday party which will be occurring downstairs momentarily. She sits in front of her mirror making her eyes look dramatic but not smoky (so that she has a defense in case Jeff calls her a whore tonight) with bright, sparkly shadow. All of a sudden, Jeff walks into the room with her back to him, and still to the side by the doorway and not just behind the mirror, so she doesn't notice.

"Hey birthday girl!"

"Jesus Christ! How the hell did you get in here?"

"It's a good thing I don't believe in Hell because I'm pretty sure that's where you'd be goin'. And your mom loves me, remember?"

"Yeah, I remember, but…"

Jeff interrupts her by walking over to her and kissing her cheek.

"I made you six cds. I asked every one of my friends what to get you, and they were all bad ideas, so this was my idea."

He hands them to her and she takes them.

"Aw, thanks. You didn't have to."

"For everything you do for me, yes I did."

"But I thought I'm a pain in the ass," she says, as more of a question.

"Yeah, but I wouldn't have it any other way. I learn a lot from it, anyway."

"So you said hi to my goldfish before you came up here, right?"

"Yup. I'll even feed him later if you want."

"Ok. Do you wanna like go back downstairs? I'll let you greet all the girls as they walk in so you can check them out."

"Someone's awfully nice tonight."

"I'm always in a giving mood around my birthday."

"I'll remember that."

"Don't. Are you just gonna stand there?"

"No. I'm gonna sit on your bed," which he proceeds to do, "and watch you play with your makeup."

"You would really rather do that than go check out all my friends without me looking?"

"You fascinate me. Besides, you're beautiful, without makeup, and I love you."

Laurel continues to apply makeup in the mirror.

"I have a feeling that tonight is going to be good."

"I want you to stay with me. I'm sick of boys ruining your life and girls causing drama in it. This is your birthday party. I want to protect you. According to me, no one has the right to mess this night up, ok?"

"They say that those you care about the most can do the most damage."

"And?"

"And maybe hanging on you is doing more damage than protecting me."

"I promise I'll be good tonight. And I'll go along with whatever you want. But I think if you stayed with me tonight, it would be amazing. It's our chance to show the world something."

"What exactly are we trying to show the world?"

"Nothing they would ever understand. But it's more for us, well actually it's mostly for you. I just, I want you to have a guy you can rely on and be with around other people and feel good about. I still feel bad about Jake."

Laurel turns to face him.

"Oh Jeff, it's not your fault."

"Well it's not yours either and you still feel pretty crappy about it....Sorry that was kind of a dumb statement I guess."

"Jeff, you're right. You can't be Jake. But if our lives continued forever with the way things are with us right now, I wouldn't complain. I was in love, Jeff. And I lost him. It happens."

"Not to any other fifteen year-old I know."

"I know, me either. Imagine how *I* feel. I'm supposed to be the expert on explaining the whole thing to people and I have no explanations. But I don't want to talk about Jake anymore. I'm sick of talking about it, but I'm especially sick of talking about it with you."

"Why?"

"Because you don't deserve it. And because I want you to know that I value what we have just as much as I value what I had with Jake. All the time I used to think about what I would do if I had to choose one of you, and how do you choose between lover and best friend? But you can't compare them."

"I know."

"But what you don't know is this. I've been thinking about that for months. And I realized who knows me better, who brings out the best in me and helps me make good choices, who I can be myself with. Who I can rely on. Who I really want to share all my milestones with. Who I would do anything with and anything for. And it's like I know we're both thinking about college and what happens with us, but not *once* have I even had that thought about Jake. You and me, Jeff, we're real. And it doesn't matter that we fight sometimes, because that's reality. And everyone who knows about us is jealous because they have this feeling about us that no matter what, we're stuck with each other forever. Which is really weird to me. I don't get how people know that."

"I know. It all seems so crazy. It's like how did this happen? How do we know how we're supposed to deal with it? How do we know if we'll ever lose each other?"

"I don't know, Jeff. I'm not worried about that. What I *am* worried about is who's walking into my house right about now, so let's go downstairs and face the world, ok?"

Jeff takes her hand and says, "Follow my lead."

Chapter 27

Ten of their friends are already downstairs playing Never Have I Ever with cards. Jeff and Laurel take a seat on the end of the couch so they can get in on this round. They listen to their friends (but whisper to each other) and put down fingers accordingly. After they hear ten things, one person is already out and everyone decides to end the game.

"Never have I ever stuffed my bra."

"Put down a finger," Laurel says to Jeff.

"This is embarrassing. You put down a finger."

"Um, I'm not the one who did it."

"*Fine.*"

"Never have I ever kissed a member of the same sex on the lips."

Jeff looks at Laurel.

"What? I haven't."

"What if I pay you?"

"Ew."

"Never have I ever been streaking."

Laurel puts down a finger, and Jeff looks at her, intrigued.

"I had to! It was a dare!"

"Never have I ever swam in the ocean or pool naked."

Laurel turns to Jeff and says, "That's what I wanna do! Can we do that someday?"

"Um, sure."

"Never have I ever smoked pot from a bong or huka."

Jeff whispers, "Not yet, anyway."

"What the hell is that supposed to mean?"

"Nevermind."

"Stop thinking you're so cool."

"Never have I ever worn sexy lingerie."

Laurel puts down a finger and she and Jeff look at each other, then she says, "Oh, come on. I'm not gonna lie in front of you."

Jeff smiles and says, "I know."

"Never have I ever acted out a sexual fantasy."

Laurel says to Jeff, "Well I know *you* haven't."

"What*ever*. Have you?"

"So far you haven't let me."

Jeff wonders if there is any truth in her sarcasm, but he is interrupted.

"Never have I ever wished for a bigger dick."

"Ok there's a finger."

"Not my fault I was born this way."

"*What*ever."

"Never have I ever played strip poker."

Jeff puts down a finger. Laurel says, "Where was I?"

"You can't be with me all the time, ok?"

Laurel looks mad.

"Never have I ever been arrested for a DUI."

The game ends. The guests at the party are talking amongst each other. Jeff and Laurel are ignoring everyone else and looking at each other. She says, "If you ever do that, I'm never talking to you again." He coughs, "Bullshit."

"Are you like *trying* to ruin my night? I thought you promised me you were gonna be good."

"You're right. I'm sorry. I just...don't ever not talk

to me, ok? Even if I do really stupid stuff when we're older."

"Jeff, we don't need to talk about this right now."

"Ok but just promise you'll never leave."

"I promise."

Laurel's best friend Kaylie yells from across the room, "Hey Laurel! Jeff and I have a surprise for you!"

Laurel whispers to him, "What the hell is this supposed to be about?"

"Oh yeah, I called Kaylie on the way here. And um, you're gonna dance with me. In front of everybody."

"Why?"

"Because. I don't know exactly what we have to prove to these people, but I know it's something."

"No, Jeff. This is what's going to happen. You're just gonna make all the girls jealous."

"So?"

"You're making them jealous of something they don't understand, and we don't either, by the way."

"Maybe not. But I know I love you. And I just want to show them that."

"And then they're gonna want you."

"Not if they're you're real friends. Besides, I wouldn't trade you for any of your friends. They probably wouldn't tolerate me as well," he kisses her cheek and takes her hand. "Now let's dance."

"K."

The guests form a circle around them while In the Arms of an Angel by Sarah Mclachlan plays and they dance. As she hears her friends say, "they're so cute," Laurel tries to pull them into the circle, but they'd rather watch her and Jeff. She whispers into his ear, "This is *so* weird."

"I think it's kinda nice."

Chapter 28

Eleventh Grade

Jeff picks up his cell phone and hears, "Hey you."

"Hey yourself. Wanna go see Lindsay Lohan's boobs?"

"Well when you put it that way...what are you talking about, anyway?"

"Mean Girls."

"You *want* to go see a chick flick? Oh right...the boobs. Yeah, ok, whatever, I'm there."

"I like you. See you at eight."

Laurel flips her cell shut, and doesn't move from the spot from the spot she had been sitting. She is puzzled.

Chapter 29

Jeff and Laurel spot each other in the parking lot of the movie theater. They walk towards each other.

"I'm freezing my balls off!"

Jeff glares at her and then begins to laugh.

"Don't *even* say a*nything*. Let's go!"

They begin to walk.

Jeff grabs her and says, "Wait! Laurel, look!"

"*What!*"

He points to woman's butt. "Baby got back!"

She laughs. She doesn't think that's funny. She just thinks he's funny. "Ok you're funny, but I really don't need to stare at other girls' butts, thank you. And I really don't want to know why *you* do...so let's go."

"Lindsay Lohan's cleavage? Sure. Let's go."

They begin to walk again.

"What am I gonna do with you?"

"I think *you* know better than *I* do."

Jeff sits next to her in the movie theater. He inches his way closer. She can't figure out why, but she can't take his eyes off him. But he won't look at her. To get his attention, she puts her hand on his knee. He doesn't flinch. Instead, he takes her hand. The movie ends and they walk out, not speaking. Laurel tries to say something, but he's got better ideas. He stands to the right and slightly behind her, cups his left hand on the back of her neck, and squeezes gently. Then he flashes her a huge smile and says, "I'll talk to you later, ok?"

Laurel looks surprised, because she is, and she knows she also looks more than content, so she smiles back and says, "K."

Chapter 30

Halloween

Jeff and Laurel are on their cell phones with each other again.

"Jeff-ey."

"What's up?"

"I got a candy-gram from a secret admirer. Was it you? Did you get someone to fill out one of those form thingies at my school?"

Jeff laughs.

"Nope. Definitely wasn't me. Sorry to disappoint."

"Very funny, but who was it?"

"Because I would know. I'm not even like friends with any guy at your school."

"Well I don't know but this is weird. Anyway oh my God the Senior Dress Up Day performances were awesome! I so don't know how we can beat that next year. There were these two guys dressed up as Mario and Luigi and they had the little car things and everything."

"That's awesome."

"Yeah, luckily I didn't have African History during lunch. Otherwise it would have been pointless since most of the class is seniors. But most of them cut class later anyway. And it's just always fun watching the seniors run around disturbing classes. This year my teachers were nice enough not have tests on Senior Dress Up Day. I still get really distracted in chem., though. But I think I'm finally learning something."

"Like what?"

"Like the atomic numbers of elements and stuff."

"Yeah, I have to have the whole thing memorized by midterms."

"I think I do, too. It's what I study in African History when she writes stuff on the board I already know until I insist on grabbing a marker and teaching it myself."

"Your teachers must *love* you."

"Well it's less work for *them*. And they do because at least I'm enthusiastic about something. I wouldn't miss that class if I was half-dead. English is killing me, though. I don't get what the point is supposed to be."

"What are you talking about?"

"It's just hard. And boring."

"Well maybe you shouldn't be taking these college-level classes."

"Well *maybe* it's how I'm going to get into a good school. Besides, your classes are harder."

"Different subjects. And in different ways. How's math?"

"Never was my favorite subject, but doable. I mean, it's fine this year. But Wellness is wicked fun. Almost every class we have to listen to the teacher read what we would do in certain situations, or like how we feel about them, and then we have to walk to one side of the room or the other or in the middle. Except there was one time when I was the only person on one side. And people from every side have to defend their position, or like explain why they're there, and it was really awkward because I had to like explain myself."

"What was it about?"

"Well we're not supposed to talk about this stuff with anyone except the people in our class. Plus it would be taking it out of context, you know what I mean? I don't know. It's not important. I just like when we get to like make lists or draw pictures in groups because it's fun and we get like to go in the hall so other groups can't see ours and stuff. And we find pictures of stuff online. And one time for one of those activities she made it so that the guys made one poster thing and the girls made another."

"What time is it?"

"Like nine. I still have so much homework to do, and I forgot to feed my fishy."

"Because *that's* time-consuming."

"No but changing his water is but I'm not gonna bother with that now. And yes actually it is because he's a slow eater and I like to watch him eat to make sure he eats. And I like to watch him swim around. It's very calming."

"You're so crazy."

"Maybe."

"How do you even know it's a boy?"

"I don't but I like boys so I like to think that."

"Like I said..." but he is interrupted.

"Shut up! I'll call you tomorrow."

"K. Don't get too stressed out."

"I won't. I already wrote about that for Wellness class, how when I'm stressed out I talk to you. Don't worry. No one reads those except our teacher."

"So what exactly *does* your class know about me?"

"Nothing. I can't tell them. I don't trust them. They're mean when they think no one's watching. And they wouldn't get it. I don't like them. They're weird."

"Aren't they supposed to be teaching you in that class not to talk like that?"

"Well it's not like I'm being mean to them. I don't have to be their best friend, ok?"

"Ok. Oh yeah, I have a game tomorrow, by the way. We can talk at like seven but then I'm gonna have to do homework, and I have a math test Friday."

"I have chem. and math quizzes like every week. Beat that."

"Don't complain.

"I'm not complaining. Just saying."

"Ok."

"But can we switch lives for a day tomorrow?"

"You wanna play in my soccer game?"

"Yeah, I guess you're right."

"I'm usually right when it comes to you."

"Yup. Ok I'll talk to you after your game tomorrow."

"Love you."

"Love you, too. Bye."

"Bye."

Chapter 31

It was almost Thanksgiving. Laurel decided that it was time to focus on something besides Jake, so she chose school. It was a choice that made many people happy, as her first quarter grades would be the best quarter grades that she ever received. She was pretty impressed with herself, as she thought that this quarter was probably as challenging as her first quarter of ninth grade had been. Of course, her success was minimal, at least in her opinion, to Jeff's. His grades were still always better, and it seemed to her that he still had time for everything else he wanted to do. It had not yet occurred to her to stop comparing herself with him and that maybe they are different in more ways than she had believed. Laurel's cell vibrates and decides she has exactly sixteen minutes to talk to Jeff before getting back to work on what she thought was an extremely boring English paper.

"Hey. I only have sixteen minutes."

"Um…are you losin' your mind just a little bit?"

"Maybe, but I have to finish this for tomorrow."

"Finish what?"

"My last paragraph of this stupid paper."

"So? How long does that take?"

"It's English class. It's important to me. I have to at least try."

"Ok…so how was your day?"

"It was good. I finally got time to think, even if it was on the treadmill during CV fitness class."

"What have you been thinking about?"

"I don't know. People. You. Oh yeah I've been working on a song for you, too."

"Really?"

"Yeah, mostly in Spanish class, and sometimes in chem. when he talks. But when we actually have to do stuff, I'm like scared of my lab partner. He's like legit. wicked sketchy. I think you need to come to my chem.. class sometime and save me."

"That bad, huh? Well, ya know…"

"I don't even want to know what you're thinking. That's gross."

"Anyway, do you want to come to Thanksgiving football with me?"

"When I could be sleeping? Have you not figured this out yet?"

"Just thought I'd ask."

"Nah. I'm good. Go with your buddies."

"We're going with girls, too."

"How cute. Like who?"

"No one you know. But um, one of them, Alex, we've been hanging out a lot."

"I see."

"Don't get all jealous on me."

"I'm not, I just don't know what you want me to say."

"What you *should* say is that you're happy I don't have to bug you every day anymore."

"Maybe I like when you bug me."

"You have an interesting way of showing it."

"Oh, Jeff. Don't give me that."

"You've been hanging out with Cameron a lot lately anyway."

"Ok I don't even know why we're having this conversation. I just know that my homework is not asexual and is not going to do itself…" she's interrupted by his laughter and then tells him to, "Shut up! I'm gonna go now."

"You know you're only saying that because you got it from me and it *is* funny."

"Anyway…"

"So, Thanksgiving?"

"I'm pretty sure my mom wants to see your ugly face for dessert."

"Ouch."

"You give me attitude, then you get it back."

"Fine, but do me a favor."

"What?"

"I want those lyrics when they're done, ok?"

"Ok."

Chapter 32

Thanksgiving break, and all that comes with it, comes and goes. They are questioned about colleges, and it seems that the biggest gossip in school, at least for juniors, revolves around SATs. Things don't exactly slow down academically, but there isn't anything major going on, and Laurel never starts studying for midterms until after Christmas break. It is the beginning of December, and Jeff is training for his first track meet of the season. He remembers something, and calls her after practice one day.

"Hey you."

"Hey, you never gave me those lyrics."

"I totally just finished it yesterday. I had to cut this tiny piece off my friendship bracelet so I thought of you and finally came up with stuff to finish writing the song."

"You mean you don't think about me all the time?"

"Nah, not really."

"That's too bad. I thought I was special."

"Oh, that you are."

"Funny."

"So how's Alex?"

"Good. I don't know. She's just a friend. I've been more focused on running lately. Our first meet is next week."

"But Alex is going, right?"

"Well…yeah, I guess. Did you have your first dance troupe practice?"

"Yeah, and I totally suck. I swear the things we do just to put on our college applications…"

"You mean the things *you* do."

"Well not all of us naturally look as good on paper as you do."

"If you're comparing us, I wouldn't put it quite like that. Besides, we're naturally better at different things."

"Which is why you should do my chem. homework."

"You'll never learn. So what are you doing this weekend?"

"Sleeping over Kaylie's. And um, we have a sweet sixteen party to go to. It's laser tag, which is totally lame."

"Could be fun. Maybe you'll meet a guy, you know, in the dark."

"Um, yeah. Sure. Maybe."

"So…homework time?"

"Yeah. At least we're reading a good book for English."

"K. Later?"

"Later."

Chapter 33

A Few Days Later

Jeff and Laurel are on their cell phones with each other again.

"Hey. How was your laser tag shindig?"

"Um…it was ok."

"Ok, what are you hiding?"

"Cameron was there."

"And…?"

"*And* he's clingy. It was weird. I was half-interested in meeting a different guy, but I couldn't because he was there."

"Now you know how I feel."

"You know what, Jeff? There's a reason for that, ok?"

"Like you get jealous."

"Yes. No. I don't know but this isn't about us."

"I'm making it about us."

"Well not everything is about us…or you. So get over yourself."

"Fine. So what are you gonna do about Cameron?"

"That really depends."

"On what?"

"On you."

"I thought this wasn't about me."

"Well it wasn't supposed to be but you have other things to do and other friends and Cameron listens to me."

"I see."

"What? Now *you're* jealous?"

"No, well maybe. I'm not exactly loving the idea of replacements."

"I'm not *replacing* you. It's more like…what's that thing with the angles from geometry?"

"Look, Cameron doesn't seem like the best guy for you to have around. He's nothing like me."

"Neither was Jake."

"Ok look, you keep Cameron at a distance, and I'll introduce you to one of my best guy friends at this party we're going to in two weekends, ok?"

"We're going to a party?"

"Yup. And you won't know anyone but me. I only know one person who's gonna be there, besides my friend I'm bringing for you. And no, you can't bring Kaylie. If things don't work out with my friend, he knows a couple other people there he can hang with, and you can be with me, dealio?"

"Um, I guess."

"Come on. It'll be fun."

"Ok fine. Dealio."

"Good girl. Now go to bed."

Chapter 34

Jeff and Laurel are at a house party. Jeff is talking with a group of guys when he sees Laurel walk in. He holds up a cup, yells "Hey!" to her from across the room, and motions for her to walk over to him, which she does. He gives her a hug while still holding his cup.

"Ok everyone," he addresses the group of guys in which he is standing, "this is my favorite girl on the planet."

"Um, Jeff," she whispers in his ear, "I think that's all they need to know for now."

"Right." he turns to the guy next to him. "Oh, so Tom, this is Laurel."

"Nice to meet you," she says and shakes his hand.

Tom says, "We were just talking about what happened in the third quarter of the Pats game last week. Did you see that? *Man* that was crazy!"

"Um, no, I...I'm more of a Red Sox fan, actually."

Tom turns to Jeff and says, "Dude, *where* did you get this chick?"

Jeff knows that Laurel could hear that and she looks annoyed so he gives her a half-smile and says to Tom, "Look, man, why don't you go check the score since you're clearly more interested in the Pats than in girls tonight."

Tom walks away and Laurel says, "*Seriously*? And you guys think *girls* are shallow?"

"He just had a little too much fun pre-gaming, and he knows you're off-limits."

"How am I *off-limits*?"

"You're not really, but evidently my friends have decided not to try to take you away from me."

"Ok…so who are all these people?"

"I don't really know, but most of the girls seem to have boyfriends who are here or they're total sluts. And I'm not interested in sluts…at least not in front of you."

"Oh. What a great courtesy."

"Yeah, well, I try."

"So what are we gonna do?"

"All the action seems to be at the bar over by the pool table. You wanna go?"

"What do I got to lose?"

"Not much with me around."

"Yup, good point. Let's go."

Chapter 35

The next morning, Laurel wakes up next to Jeff. They are on a couch. Jeff wakes up because a hand slipped into his jeans pocket. He opens his eyes and sees Laurel smiling at him, but he has to remember where he is and why she's there. Finally, he says, "Hey."

"Hey."

"Um, what's with the pocket?"

"Oh. The song. I forgot to give it you, but now I remembered."

"Oh. I forgot how beautiful you are, and I'm sorry I forgot to tell you last night."

"*Wow* that is good considering it's nine in the morning and you went to bed at five."

"Yeah, well...hey what happened to Tom?"

"I opened the bathroom door and saw him making out with some girl. He left before we went to sleep."

"You look like something's wrong."

"No, I'm fine."

"Well you look different...where is everyone?"

"Oh, um, there were only a few people left and they all went to sleep upstairs so we got left here."

"Oh."

He took her in his arms, and they went back to sleep. For three hours. He didn't know that he had what she needed to get better. He had the missing part. She didn't know that he had a hole in his heart. For three hours, these breathing bodies were somewhat together somewhere. They slept, and while they were asleep, their souls left their bodies and did not come back. The bodies stopped breathing. Two hearts stopped beating. Teenagers wandered to a finished basement to find the corpses. One girl fainted. Paramedics arrived within minutes, but it was way too late. Later it would be discovered that they had both been poisoned.

When they woke up, they drank the juice on the coffee table next to them, before going back to sleep forever. It was the collective effort and planning of those who were jealous, a bunch of whom had slept upstairs. One of them planted the juice after they saw that Jeff and Laurel were asleep. They all got away with murder because they had planned the whole thing, including their lies for the police, very well. Jeff and Laurel were dead, but their souls were still together. They were destined to be together forever. Their families did not know that, not quite like they did, but they knew that there was something special about their relationship. That is why once Jeff put them on their wrists, their friendship bracelets were never removed.

CPSIA information can be obtained at www.ICGtesting.com
Printed in the USA
BVOW012157020113

309620BV00001B/33/P